HELLO, I'M THEA!

I'm *Geronimo Stilton*'s sister. As I'm sure you know from my brother's bestselling novels, I'm a special correspondent for *The Rodent's Gazette*, Mouse Island's most famouse newspaper. Unlike my 'fraidy mouse brother, I absolutely adore traveling, having adventures, and meeting rodents from all around the world!

The adventure I want to tell you about begins at Mouseford Academy, the school I went to when I was a young mouseling. I had such a great experience there as a student that I came back to teach a journalism class.

When I returned as a grown mouse, I met five really special students: Colette, Nicky, Pamela, Paulina, and Violet. You could hardly imagine five more different mouselings, but they became great friends right away. And they liked me so much that they decided to name their group after me: the Thea Sisters! I was so touched by that, I decided to write about their adventures. So turn the page to read a fabumouse adventure about the

THEA SISTERS!

NICKY

Name: Nicky
Nickname: Nic
Home: Australia
Secret ambition: Wants to be an ecologist.
Loves: Open spaces and nature.
Strengths: She is always in a good mood, as long as she's outdoors!
Weaknesses: She can't sit still!
Secret: Nicky is claustrophobic — she can't stand being in small, tight places.

COLETTE

Name: Colette

Nickname: It's Colette, please. (She can't stand nicknames.)

Home: France

Secret ambition: Colette is very particular about her appearance. She wants to be a fashion writer.

Loves: The color pink.

Strengths: She's energetic and full of great ideas.

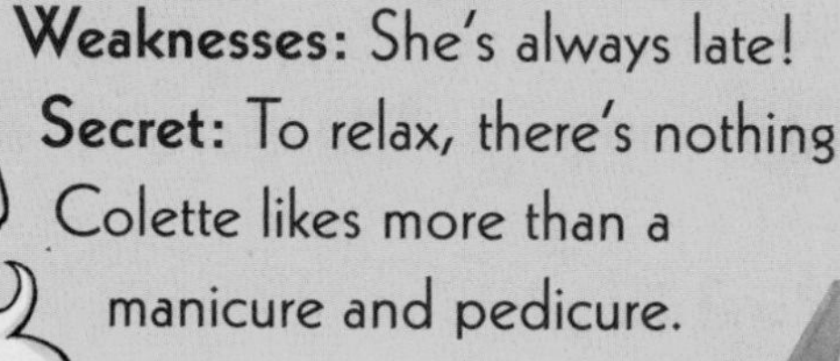

Weaknesses: She's always late!

Secret: To relax, there's nothing Colette likes more than a manicure and pedicure.

VIOLET

Name: Violet
Nickname: Vi
Home: China
Secret ambition: Wants to become a great violinist.
Loves: Books! She is a real intellectual, just like my brother, Geronimo.
Strengths: She's detail-oriented and always open to new things.
Weaknesses: She is a bit sensitive and can't stand being teased. And if she doesn't get enough sleep, she can be a real grouch!

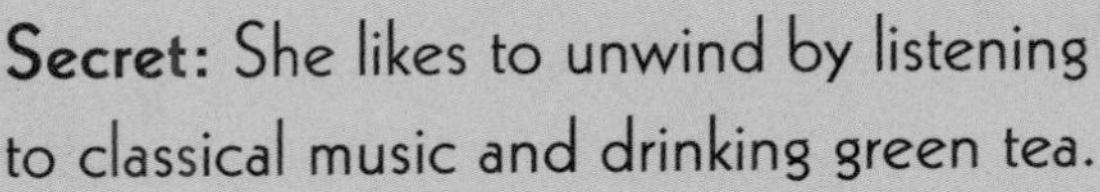

Secret: She likes to unwind by listening to classical music and drinking green tea.

PAULINA

Name: Paulina
Nickname: Polly
Home: Peru
Secret ambition: Wants to be a scientist.
Loves: Traveling and meeting people from all over the world. She is also very close to her sister, Maria.
Strengths: Loves helping other rodents.
Weaknesses: She's shy and can be a bit clumsy.
Secret: She is a computer genius!

PAMELA

Name: Pamela

Nickname: Pam

Home: Tanzania

Secret ambition: Wants to become a sports journalist or a car mechanic.

Loves: Pizza, pizza, and more pizza! She'd eat pizza for breakfast if she could.

Strengths: She is a peacemaker. She can't stand arguments.

Weaknesses: She is very impulsive.

Secret: Give her a screwdriver and any mechanical problem will be solved!

Geronimo Stilton

Thea Stilton AND THE STAR CASTAWAYS

Scholastic Inc.

New York Toronto London Auckland
Sydney Mexico City New Delhi Hong Kong

ISBN 978-0-545-22774-2

Based on an original idea by Elisabetta Dami.

www.geronimostilton.com

Published by Scholastic Inc., 557 Broadway, New York, NY 10012.

Text by Thea Stilton
Original title *I naufraghi delle stelle*
Cover by Arianna Rea, Daniela Geremia, and Ketty Formaggio
Illustrations by Alessandro Battan, Sergio Cabella, Paolo Ferrante, Daniela Geremia, Sonia Matrone, Marco Mazzarello, Roberta Pierpaoli, Arianna Rea, Maurizio Roggerone, and Roberta Tedeschi
Color by Tania Boccalini, Alessandra Bracaglia, Concetta Daidone, Ketty Formaggio, and Micaela Tangorra
Graphics by Paola Cantoni, with assistance from Michela Battaglin

Special thanks to Beth Dunfey
Translated by Julia Heim
Interior design by Kay Petronio

12 11 10 9 8 7 6 5 11 12 13 14 15 16/0

Printed in the U.S.A. 40
First printing, June 2011

HOLEY STRING CHEESE!

When I scampered off the airplane during my last layover before reaching New Mouse City, I had only one thing on my mind: **getting** home!

Oh, pardon me. I haven't introduced myself yet. My name is THEA STILTON, and I'm a special correspondent for The Rodent's Gazette, the most famouse newspaper on Mouse Island.

I had been on the road for more than a month. I'd **TRAVELED** far and wide across the Gobi Desert, in an SUV and on

GOBI DESERT
This enormous desert in central Asia extends about 500,000 square miles. The majority of the desert is arid and rocky — only a small portion is sandy.

a camel's back. It was a fabumouse trip, but verrrry exhausting!

While I was waiting for my flight to New Mouse City, I sat down to watch the news. Suddenly, what do you think I saw on the TV? The smiling snouts of the THEA SISTERS!

"Holey string cheese with Swiss on top!" I exclaimed. "It's really them! Colette, Nicky, PAMELA, PAULINA, and **Violet**!"

They were all wearing space suits, even the usually fashionable Colette. It was clear they were about to leave for a trip to the moon!

"For the love of sliced cheddar!" I cried. I was so excited I was squeaking out loud. The other rodents in the waiting area all looked at me like the **cheese** had slipped off my **cracker**.

"Pardon me," I muttered. I was so embarrassed! "You see, those mice were my students at **MOUSEFORD ACADEMY**!"

I could still hardly believe what I was seeing. Since the moment I met Colette, Nicky, PAMELA, PAULINA, and **Violet**, they've **AMAZED** me with their **adventures** around the world, and now

they were about to blast *out* of this world on a trip to **space**!

I was **excited** for them, but I was also a little **NERVOUS**. So I pulled out my cell phone and called OCTAVIUS DE MOUSUS, the headmaster of Mouseford Academy.

He confirmed that it was true: My five young friends were headed to the moon! "Colette, Nicky, PAMELA, PAULINA, and **Violet** asked me to tell you that they'll share all the **details** with you when they return!"

Of course, that's exactly what they did. So now, dear readers, I can share the most EXTRAORDINARY adventure of the THEA SISTERS!

READY FOR ORBIT?

It all began a month earlier. . . .

Professor Mousilda Marblemouse, the modern languages teacher at Mouseford Academy, had asked Paulina to bring the Thea Sisters to meet her in the COMPUTER lab. It was ten at night, a strange hour for such a request! But Professor Marblemouse had been unusually mysterious, so the mouselets hurried over to meet her. The professor was always looking for new and STIMULATING PROJECTS for her students: Who knew what she had in mind?

"They say curiosity killed the cat, but this

time it might get me, too!" exclaimed Pam.

At that hour, the **big** lab was almost empty. Only the professor and the headmaster were there, sitting in front of a large **COMPUTER** screen. They were videoconferencing with a mouse with thick white *whiskers* and friendly eyes under **BUSHY** eyebrows.

Paulina recognized him immediately. "That's Napoleon Smith, the **billionaire**!"

As soon as he heard those words, Mr. Smith *smiled* and said hello. "Here they

NAPOLEON SMITH

Napoleon Smith is an ingenious businessmouse and a very wealthy inventor. What's his secret for staying on top? He's got a **snout for business** and a **mouseling's enthusiasm** for unusual adventures!

are, finally, the famouse THEA SISTERS! Mousilda has told me WONDERFUL things about you, mouselets, and I have big news for you. You've been selected for a trip to orbit the moon!"

Colette, Nicky, PAMELA, PAULINA, and **Violet** felt as if the BREATH had been knocked out of them!

"Who, us?" gasped Violet, looking behind her as if some other rodents might have followed them into the lab.

"Yes, you!" said Professor Marblemouse, smiling warmly. The mouselets later discovered that she and Napoleon Smith were OLD friends. He had always held his pal from MOUSEFORD ACADEMY in high esteem, so he turned to her after he'd created a **space travel agency**!

Napoleon Smith began to explain his

project. "Businessmice have been dreaming of this for quite a while! However, I am the only one ready to take tourists in search of EXCITEMENT to **ORBIT** the moon! The first voyagers will depart in a month. The whole world will be talking about it! It will be a fantastic adventure, with a publicity launch that's out of this world!"

"I imagine that this first **trip** will determine the success of the entire venture,"

PROFESSOR DE MOUSUS put in.

"That's right!" admitted the billionaire. With increasing passion, he continued to explain. "That's why I want the world's most famouse journalists there: Greta Van Rodenten, Ricky Newsmouse, and Ian Focus!"

Pamela and Nicky JUMPED.

"Kissing kangaroo kittens!" Nicky exclaimed. She and the other mouselets were devoted READERS of the reporting team Newsmouse and Focus. Ricky Newsmouse's articles were real works of SKILL and an

JOURNALISM

Journalism is the art of reporting and writing about current events. Reporters are journalists who describe the facts they've uncovered during the course of their investigations. Journalists often write for websites, newspapers, and magazines, or report stories on television.

THE MOON

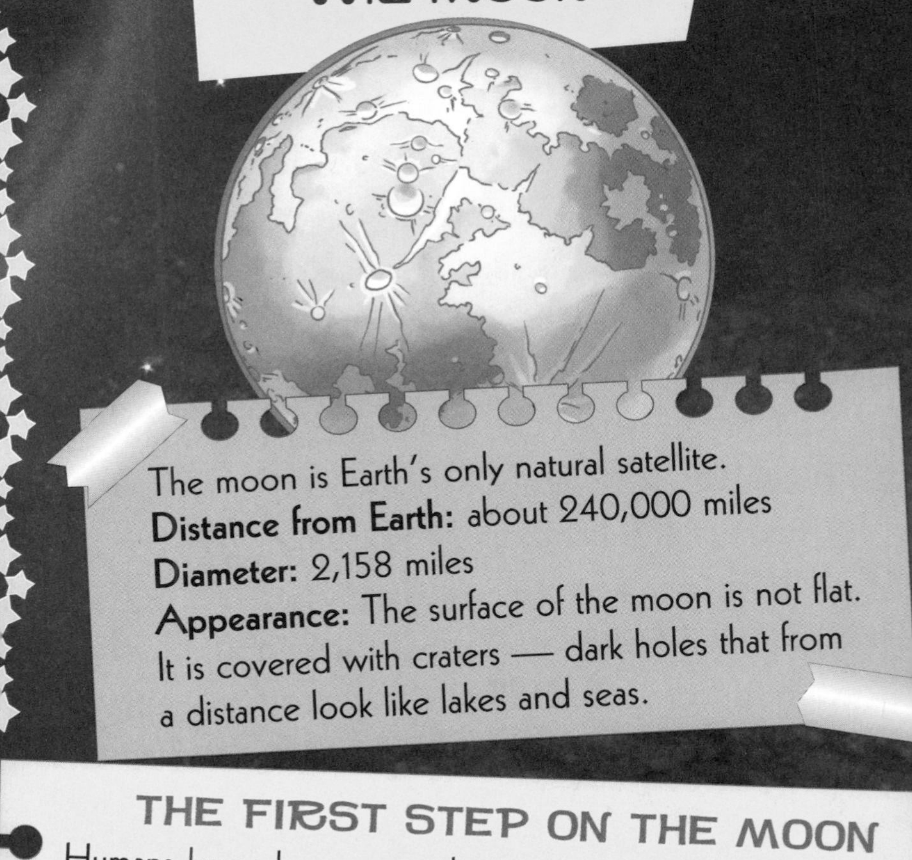

The moon is Earth's only natural satellite.
Distance from Earth: about 240,000 miles
Diameter: 2,158 miles
Appearance: The surface of the moon is not flat. It is covered with craters — dark holes that from a distance look like lakes and seas.

THE FIRST STEP ON THE MOON

Humans have always wanted to go to the moon, and this dre became a reality on **July 20, 1969**. The first astronaut to set fo on the moon was Neil Armstrong, followed by Buzz Aldrin abo twenty minutes later.

Today most astronauts don't travel to the moon. NASA (th National Aeronautics and Space Administration) is focused o exploration far beyond the moon. But many scientists think the moo could be a valuable base for exploration of planets such as Mars.

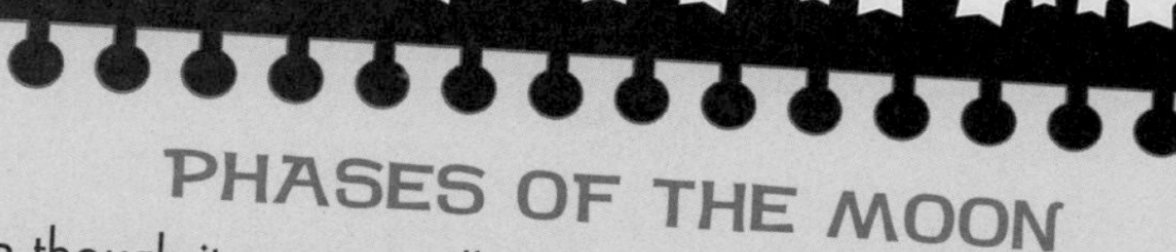

PHASES OF THE MOON

Even though it seems to illuminate the night sky, the moon does not give off light — it reflects light from the sun. If you gaze at the moon a few nights in a row, you'll see that it doesn't always look the same: Its face can be completely illuminated, completely dark, or lit up only in part. As the moon orbits Earth, we see different portions of its sunlit side. These are called the **phases** of the moon.

When the moon is between the sun and Earth, we see the side that faces away from the sun. Therefore, the moon appears dark. This phase is called the **new moon**.

When the moon is opposite the sun and its lit side faces Earth, we have a **full moon**.

After a new moon, the illuminated portion of the moon grows, and we say that it is "**waxing**." After the moon is full, the portion of the moon that's lit up is gradually reduced, and we say that he Moon is "**waning**." t takes 29.5 days for the noon to complete one unar cycle.

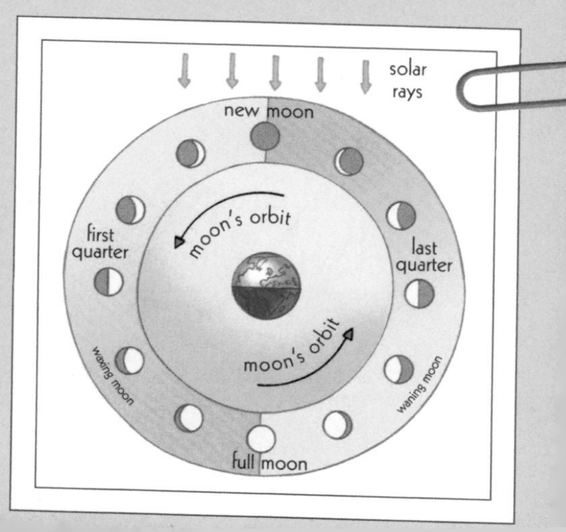

example for all journalism students. As for Ian Focus's photos, they were so **beautiful** they often expressed more than words could!

Colette's snout LIT UP when she heard Greta Van Rodenten's name. Colette was a big fan of the **Mouse TV** television journalist.

"But that's not all!" continued Napoleon Smith. "I also want fresh-snouted young journalists, rodents full of **enthusiasm** for an exceptional undertaking like this one, to join our expedition **UP THERE**."

A shiver of surprise and excitement went through all five THEA SISTERS.

After a moment, Paulina found her squeak again. She stuttered, "And . . . w-we are the o-ones you've chosen?"

Napoleon Smith clapped his paws. "Welcome aboard, mouselings!"

CLAP CLAP CLAP!!!

A TOP SECRET BASE

The THEA SISTERS barely had enough time to pack their bags and say good-bye to their classmates. Napoleon Smith wanted them at his moon preparation base as soon as possible. It was located on a remote island in **MICRONESIA**.

Before the five mouselets left for **SPACE**, they had to pass extensive medical exams and **RIGOROUS** physical training. There was much work to be done!

MICRONESIA

Micronesia is made up of **more than 600 islands,** which span a vast area of the Pacific Ocean. The name Micronesia comes from two Greek words that together mean "small islands." Politically, Micronesia is divided into four independent states.

FIONA

Right after breakfast the next day, a **helicopter** landed on Whale Island and picked up the **mouselets**. It flew them to the New Mouse City airport, where Napoleon Smith's private **JET** was waiting. The jet would take them directly to the moon preparation base!

Fiona, Napoleon Smith's personal **assistant**, met them at the airport. She was small and **energetic**, with a smiley snout that immediately made the THEA SISTERS feel at ease.

"Howdy!" she said cheerfully. "Please, sit wherever you like! The plane is all yours. Would you like something to **EAT**?"

Pam perked up immediately. "Ooh, do you have **pizza**?"

"Pam, we just ate!" said Colette.

"Sure, but what if the pizza in space isn't as good as the stuff here on Earth?" Pam asked earnestly.

The mouselets all laughed.

Paulina turned to Fiona. "Could you tell me where exactly the ISLAND we're going to is located? I looked for it on a map, but I couldn't find it."

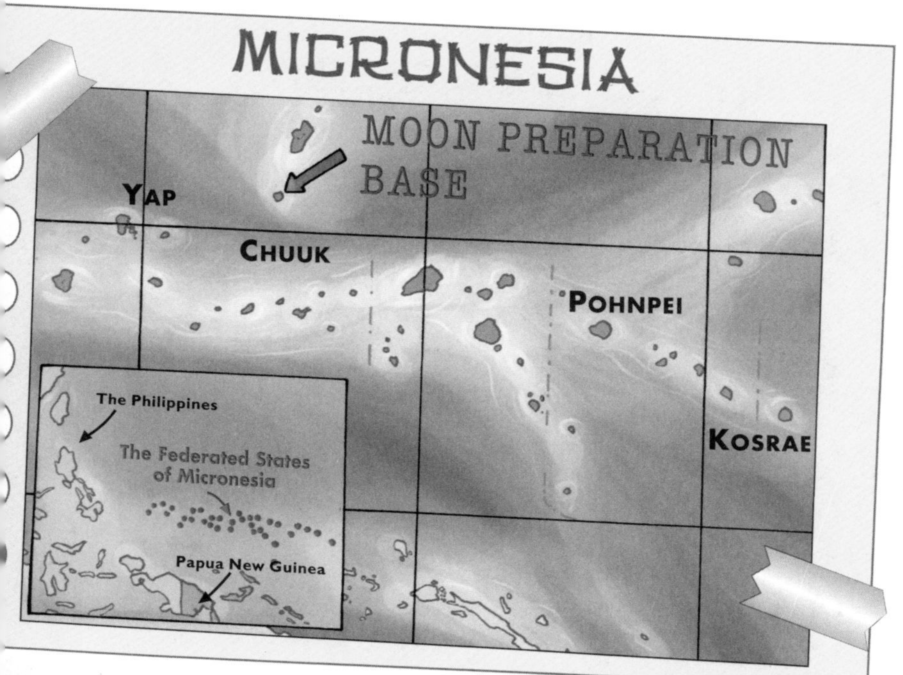

"It is one of hundreds of islands in **MICRONESIA**," explained Fiona. "It isn't marked in atlases, only on **navigational** maps. The island is Mr. Smith's private property. He doesn't want anyone sticking their snouts into his business." She noticed Paulina's **bewildered** expression and explained, "**Space** tourism is a billion-dollar business. It is very important that Mr. Smith's competitors don't get their paws on his project's trade **SECRETS**!"

ORBITAL FLIGHT

Outer space is considered one of the most promising tourist frontiers. So far, only the Russian Federal Space Agency has offered orbital flights (that is, flights around Earth). But private companies in the United States, Great Britain, and Germany are also pursuing the idea.

WELCOME! WELCOME!

After a LOOOOOOOONG flight, the plane began to descend. The sun was setting over the Pacific. The Thea Sisters admired the infinite stretch of TURQUOISE ocean, which was flecked with red and gold SPARKLES from the sunlight.

As land drew nearer, the mouselets were able to make out many small green islands, white BEACHES, and PALM TREES.

"But I don't see any houses!" observed Violet.

"Only some of the islands in Micronesia are inhabited. Many of the islands are too small to live on," explained Fiona. "Ah, here we are at last! Look down. . . . There it is!"

The THEA SISTERS crowded around the

window to get a better look. They saw a distant shape that soon became a FLAME-COLORED hill. Then a glass building in the shape of a pyramid came into view. It reflected the colors of the sunset.

"Gorgeous, isn't it?" said Fiona with pride. "Okay, we'd better buckle our seat belts until we've LANDED!"

When they scampered off the plane, Napoleon Smith was waiting for them. But he wasn't alone. Right at his side were . . .

"ROBOTS?!?" exclaimed Paulina. She was a bit of a computer whiz, and she loved anything involving new technology. "Are those really robots next to Mr. Smith?"

"You bet!" confirmed Fiona, laughing. "There are four different types of robots on the island. We have some of the most advanced TECHNOLOGY in the world."

Napoleon Smith looked HAPPY to see them. He gave each of the mouselets a lovely flower necklace. As he did, his robots greeted them: "**Welcome!**"

"At last our group of courageous astromice is complete!" exclaimed the billionaire, rubbing his paws together with satisfaction.

Fiona whispered something to him. "Oh, I'm getting more absentminded than my great-aunt Lazybrain!" Mr. Smith said. "I forgot the most **important** thing!"

He reached into his pocket and pulled out five small identical gadgets. They looked like large metal buttons. Each had a GROOVED center surrounded by lots of little stars.

Fiona took the gadgets and gave them to the THEA SISTERS.

"These are your communicators. Be sure not to lose them! You can use them to open the doors to your rooms and give SIMPLE voice commands to the robots."

"Whoa! Just like on MOUSE TREK," said Nicky, looking awed.

"How do you use them?" asked Paulina. looking inquisitively at the communicator.

"Just brush your paw against it like this and then tell the robot what you want it to do," said Fiona, demonstrating. "The robots won't UNDERSTAND your words unless you use the communicator, so you should wear it all the time."

Fiona noticed the anxious EXPRESSION on Colette's snout. "Colette, I know a fashion mouse like you is worried about ruining your pretty SWEATER . . . but don't be! These communicators use the latest generation of adhesives. They'll stick to any type of fabric without using a pin, and they won't leave holes, I promise."

Together, the little group headed toward the GIANT glass pyramid. The space inside was incredibly vast and filled with light.

"Holey cheese!" Colette, Nicky, Pamela, Paulina, and Violet exclaimed in unison.

Napoleon smiled proudly. "I'm happy you like it. And this is just the beginning of the wonders you'll see! But now I bet you're tired and need to catch your BREATH. My robots will show you to your rooms. In a few hours Fiona and I will take you to dinner, and then you can finally meet your fellow astromice!"

LET ME INTRODUCE THE THEA SISTERS!

As promised, that evening Napoleon Smith hosted a *fancy* dinner to introduce the Thea Sisters to their fellow travelers. The first rodent they met was Professor Sebastian Golden. "He is the director of the **space** center and my right paw!" said Napoleon Smith with pride. "If I am the **heart** of this project, he is the brains!"

PROFESSOR GOLDEN

The professor is the **director** of Napoleon Smith's entire space project. He is the one who translates Mr. Smith's ingenious ideas into reality. Anything Mr. Smith dreams up, Professo Golden makes happen!

The professor didn't squeak a word, but he shook the mouselets' paws one by one. He was a tall, thin rodent with tight lips and a severe expression.

In almost every way, the professor seemed to be Mr. Smith's opposite. As Napoleon led the mouselets away, he whispered, "The professor looks like a grump, but his mind is sharper than a block of CHEDDAR. We have worked together for ten years!"

Next, Mr. Smith brought the THEA SISTERS to a table where three rodents wearing suits and ties were seated. They were working out mysterious equations on their calculators at an impressive speed.

"These are Rice, Watermouse, and Hooper, three big INVESTORS interested in my project," whispered Napoleon. "They know more about business than my great-uncle Moneybags! It

RICE, WATERMOUSE, AND HOOPER

They are three businessmice who have invested in Mr. Smith's moon mission. That' why they're so busy with calculations and estimates!

is very **important** that they finance future **flights**. That's why I invited them."

Next, Napoleon Smith led the five mouselets to the table of **JOURNALISTS**.

"I'm so excited, my tail is **trembling**!" Colette whispered.

Napoleon Smith greeted the journalists. Then, he said: "May I present your five **young** colleagues: *Colette*, *Nicky*, PAMELA, PAULINA, and **Violet**!"

"Oh, no, we are just **students** at **MOUSEFORD ACADEMY**!" Pamela said hastily. "We're really **big** fans!"

Ricky Newsmouse thanked her warmly.

"It's an honor to meet you!" Nicky said. "I always read your pieces. It's my dream to visit and write about the most remote places on Earth, just like you!"

"What's the point of describing something with words when the IMAGES speak for themselves, right, Greta?" Ian Focus interrupted.

Greta Van Rodenten nodded eagerly.

Focus sounded defensive, and Nicky was taken aback. But from the WINK he gave her, she quickly realized that the challenge was not for her but for Newsmouse.

RICKY NEWSMOUSE AND IAN FOCUS

Ricky Newsmouse (writer) and Ian Focus (photographer) are a famouse and established **reporting team**.

The look Focus shot his reporting partner was **colder** than ice.

Newsmouse's response was equally **chilly**. "They didn't award us for our photos, but for our **investigation**, right, Greta?"

Again, the TV journalist agreed.

The mouselets exchanged glances, puzzled. Why were Newsmouse and Focus sniping at each other? And why was Greta Van Rodenten encouraging them?

"Without my PHOTOS, no one would have read your reports!" retorted Focus.

"And without my WORDS, your photos would never have been published!" Newsmouse shot back.

At that point, Greta Van Rodenten intervened with a chuckle. "Words and pictures . . . they've been at war since journalism was invented! Who knows which will win this latest battle?"

The THEA SISTERS were feeling a little AWKWARD, so they quickly took their seats at the table. Pam sighed. "What a disappointment! I thought Newsmouse and Focus went together like CHEESE and crackers, and instead . . ."

". . . they're fighting like cats and RATS! I am afraid those two won't last long together!" concluded Nicky SADLY.

GRETA VAN RODENTEN: JOURNALIST OF THE YEAR!

GRETA VAN RODENTEN

Greta is a **television personality** who became successful thanks to her charm and her assertive style.

ZERO GRAVITY

The next morning, Colette, Nicky, PAMELA, PAULINA, and **Violet** got up early. They had to go through extensive **medical exams**.

Before setting out on a **trip** to the moon, they had to be sure they were in **TIP-TOP** shape.

In the afternoon, Napoleon Smith had a surprise for them. "And now, mouselings, we **FLY**!" he declared.

They headed toward the runway, where a plane was waiting for them.

"Where are we going?" asked Paulina.

"Well, first we'll go up, then down, and perhaps a bit of side to side as well," answered the billionaire, chuckling under his *whiskers*.

The mouselets looked at one another in confusion. But no matter how many questions they asked, Mr. Smith refused to say anything more.

As soon as the plane reached cruising ALTITUDE, Mr. Smith invited the Thea Sisters to follow him into another cabin. It was empty, with white padded walls.

"Help! What's happening?!" cried Colette. "I feel like I'm floating away!"

In fact, all five mouselets could feel their paws leaving the ground.

Violet, Paulina, and Nicky clutched one another, FRIGHTENED.

"Surprise!" shouted Mr. Smith. "We are in ZERO gravity, just like in space!"

The feeling of weightlessness lasted for only a few moments; then both he and the mouselets TUMBLED onto the padded

floor. For about thirty seconds, they had been completely without **gravity**!

"Pretty cool, right?" said Mr. Smith, getting to his paws.

"**Fabumouse!**" declared Nicky. "But you should have told us earlier. That way we could have had some fun, too!"

Mr. Smith apologized, but he couldn't help **laughing**. "I'm sorry! But don't worry, you're about to get a second chance. Get ready: Soon we're going to fly again!"

PARABOLIC FLIGHTS

Parabolic flights are used to achieve zero gravity. To get the right effect, a plane must fly **24,000 to 32,000** feet above the ground, then go into a steep nosedive before flying upward again, drawing a parabola. For about a minute, while the plane is descending, the passengers feel weightless. **NASA** uses the technique to train astronauts.

SPIDER-BOTS!

The next few days were intense. The THEA SISTERS and their fellow astromice had to learn how to move without gravity while wearing BULKY suits covered with computerized sensors.

Even getting dressed proved to be unusual! Pamela shrieked when she saw some MECHANICAL spiders climbing up the legs of her space suit.

"They are very useful robots," Napoleon Smith explained. "Wearing a space suit is very complicated. With so many cables, tubes, and attachments to set up, even the smallest MISTAKE can cause trouble. These mini-robots are REALLY FAST and very smart. Using them is the most efficient way to make sure you astromice stay safe!"

Violet took one in her paw. "I think they're cute!" she said, stroking it as gently as if it were her pet cricket, **Frilly**.

Colette observed the **MINI-ROBOT** carefully. "It's not bad-looking . . . but it could use a makeover!" She reached into her purse and pulled out some furclips decorated with small flowers and pom-poms. She put them on the robots. "From frumpy to fabumouse!"

Once the mouselets were all zipped up inside

Space Walks

PRESSURE

The moon does not have its own atmosphere or oxygen To explore it, human beings must bring their own environment with them. Astronauts wear pressurized space suits that completely cover their bodies. The suits provide oxygen, protection from cold or heat, and even water for the astronauts to drink.

PRESSURIZATION

Pressurization is an operation that maintains the environment at a pressure the human body can withstand.

PRESSURIZED SUITS

On spaceships, there are systems that control the atmosphere, allowing the astronauts to move around without their space suits. During takeoff and landing, however, there is always a risk that the ship will lose pressure, so astronauts must wear their pressurized suits. Each suit is built specifically for the astronaut who will wear it.

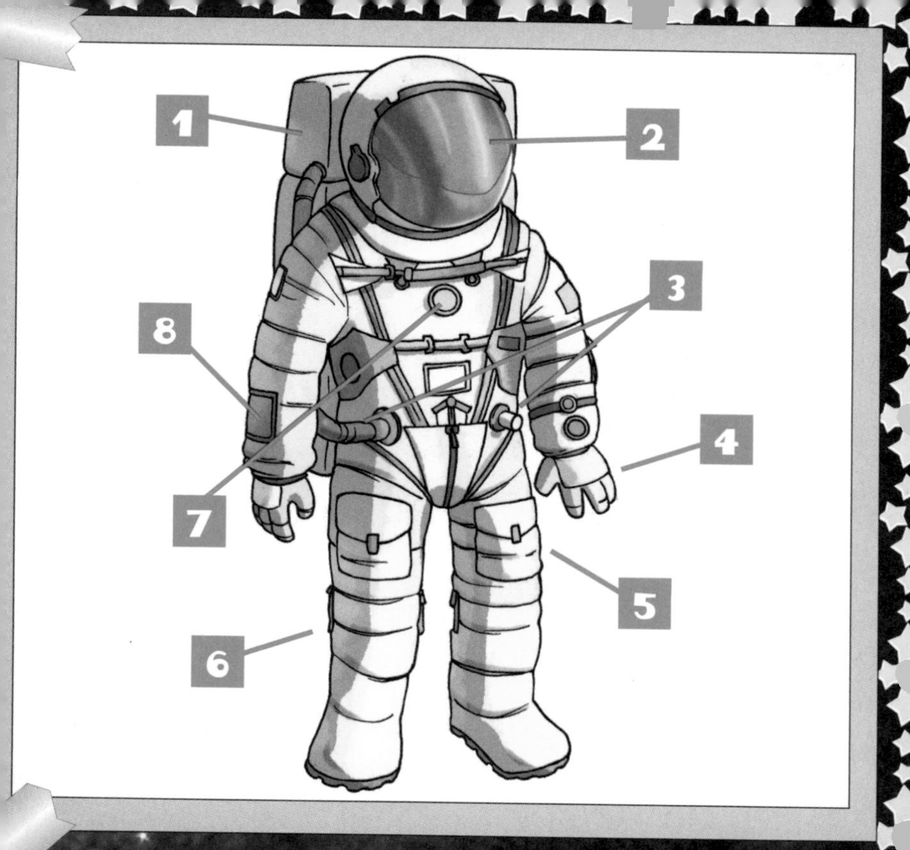

1	Primary Life Support Subsystem, which includes an oxygen tank	5	Multipurpose pocket
2	Helmet	6	Lower torso, which includes pants and boots
3	Tether and cord for cooling system	7	Control panel for the space suit and the Primary Life Support Subsystem
4	EVA (extravehicular activity) gloves, which are made to keep the astronaut's fingers warm and movable	8	Cuff checklist, to remind astronauts of their tasks in space

their suits, the eleven astromice headed for a large swimming **pool**. According to their instructors, going underwater was the best way to get used to moving in **zero gravity**.

The THEA SISTERS jumped in first. But Mr. Rice, Mr. Watermouse, and Mr. Hooper hesitated at their turn.

"Well, don't be scared to get your **FUR** wet! Come on in," Ricky Newsmouse said, encouraging them. He turned to Ian Focus. "Looks like we've finally found three bigger 'FRAIDY CATS than you!"

Focus was stung. "Well, don't forget the time we were working on that skydiving story," he reminded **Newsmouse**. "You were **afraid** to open your own parachute, so you grabbed my tail instead!"

Greta laughed and put her paw over Focus's. "Oh, you two! I don't know how

you've managed to get along **ALL THESE YEARS**."

At that moment, Mr. Rice, Mr. Hooper, and Mr. Watermouse took the **PLUNGE**.

"They probably got tired of the bickering!" Nicky whispered to her friends.

"I was checking my favorite media blog last night, and there are rumors that Greta Van Rodenten wants to break up **Focus** and **Newsmouse**!" Paulina replied.

"**BUT WHY?**" asked Pam.

"Maybe she wants to work with one of them," Paulina answered.

"I don't believe it!" said Colette. She didn't think that her hero would do something so **low-down** and calculating.

"Let's keep an **EYE** on the situation and see what happens," said Violet.

Nicky nodded. "I'd hate to see such a great team of journalists break up."

THE STARCRUISE

After several weeks of training, the moment finally arrived to visit the shuttle that would take Napoleon Smith and his guests into SPACE. The thirteen-member crew of the EXPEDITION, including Professor Golden and Napoleon Smith, climbed aboard the *Starcruise*, a brand-new SPACESHIP. Unlike most spacecraft, this one could land at a normal airport and be ready for a new mission within just a few hours!

The THEA SISTERS were really excited. As for Napoleon Smith, he was so excited he seemed ten years younger!

Even the three investors were enthusiastic. For the first time in weeks, they left their CALCULATORS in their rooms.

The only ones who seemed unmoved by all

the excitement were Ricky Newsmouse and Ian Focus, who continued **competing** for the attention of Greta Van Rodenten.

The interior of the *Starcruise* was both sleek and comfortable. It had been conceived by a famouse Italian **designer**. Even the **sophisticated** Greta *ooh*ed and *aah*ed in appreciation when she saw it. "Oh, Ian, will you get a picture of me sitting in this splendid spacecraft!" she **EXCLAIMED**. "It could be the cover of our travel **BOOK**. What do you think?"

"Fabumouse!" he replied, getting shots from all angles.

Newsmouse pretended not to hear, but Paulina noticed that his

tail was twitching with irritation. "I'm starting to think that blog is right — she's definitely trying to split up Newsmouse and Focus!" she whispered to Colette.

Colette nodded sadly. "It sure seems that way." She sighed.

Meanwhile, Nicky was starting to feel a little queasy. The closed space, the suit, the **helmet**, the tight seat belt — it was all too much for her. You see, Nicky is claustrophobic — she can't stand being in small, NARROW spaces! She quickly took off her helmet and loosened her seat belt, and she immediately felt better. She was very DETERMINED: She didn't want anyone to call her a 'FRAIDY MOUSE!

"Oh, don't worry about that!" Napoleon Smith said, smiling at her. "Why, my great-uncle Dizzypaws suffered terribly from claustrophobia! So you see, your experience is very valuable to me. This problem will surely come up again, when we make the moon trips available to tourists. We need to find a solution!"

"I've got a solution!" Pamela interrupted. "I propose we go eat! It's practically lunchtime."

Everyone agreed eagerly, except for Greta, who rolled her EYES and muttered, "This is what happens when you let amateurs tag along with the pros."

Violet frowned. "What's with that rodent?"

Nicky shook her snout. "I don't know. She has a flea in her fur about something!"

EIGHT AND A HALF MINUTES

After another week of preparation, the little expedition was finally ready to blast off!

It was a clear day with very little wind, ideal for the *Starcruise*'s liftoff. The astromice split into groups and scampered onto the **ELEVATOR** that would take them on board.

Paulina turned for one last **look** at the glass pyramid and saw Fiona waving good-bye. Then she and the other mouselets took their places on the ship. Everyone was a little quieter than usual.

"I can't believe we're really heading into space!" Nicky whispered.

The other mouselets nodded.

"Of all the adventures we've had, this has got to be the most THRILLING!" Pam replied.

A few minutes later, the ship began to VIBRATE. At first, the shaking was hardly noticeable, and then it slowly got STRONGER and STRONGER.

"Don't get your tails in a twist, my friends!" Napoleon Smith squeaked. "The *Starcruise* is telling us that it's ready to go! Bon voyage!"

READY, SET, GO!

Earth's **atmosphere** is a blanket of air that surrounds the planet. It reaches about 350 miles from the surface, and it serves many functions, including absorbing energy from the sun and protecting us from the freezing temperatures of space. It takes about eight and a half minutes for a space shuttle to blast off Earth and go into orbit.

The countdown began!

Ten . . . nine . . . eight . . . seven . . . six . . . five . . . four . . . three . . . two . . . one . . . **BLAST OFF**!

The *Starcruise* continued to accelerate. And the pressure the ASTROMICE felt on their chests grew greater and greater. Despite the trial runs they had done all month, it was impossible to stay **calm**!

"Eight and a half minutes! Just eight and a half minutes . . . ," Colette repeated to herself. Professor Golden had told them that it took eight and a half minutes to get free of Earth's pull. After that, the **ENGINES** would be turned off.

"It feels more like eight and a half *hours*!" Violet moaned.

Then, suddenly . . . there was silence!

The motors had stopped, and the feeling of heaviness vanished. Almost immediately, the passengers felt a great sense of lightness.

"Yeah!" yelled Pam, unbuckling her seat belt. Nicky immediately followed her example. The other astromice did the same. They all began to FLOAT through the air!

Focus started flapping his arms up and down. "This must be what it feels like to be a bird!" he exclaimed.

Colette, Paulina, and Violet gazed out the window at Earth below: It was so beautiful!

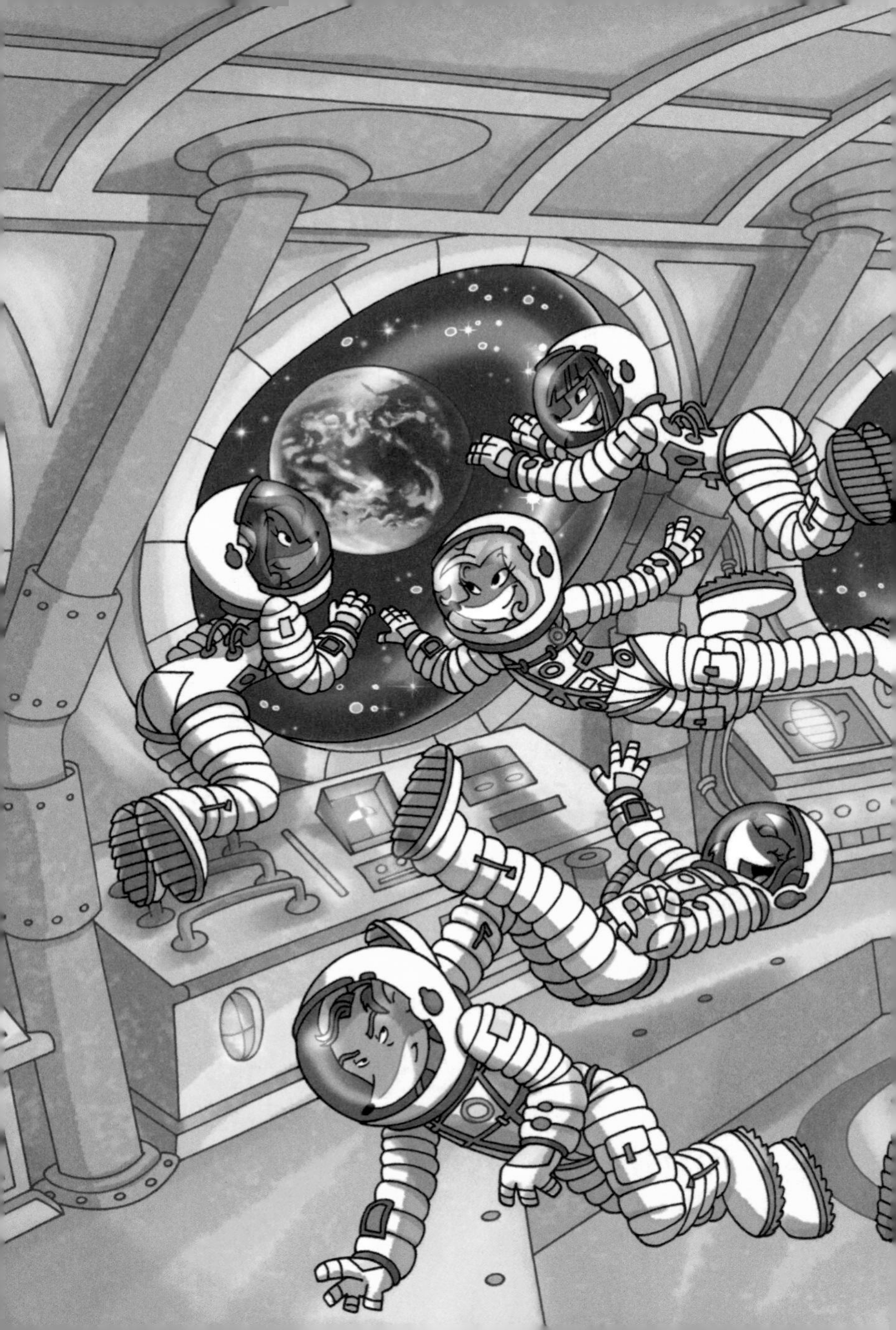

From here, they could see white streaks of clouds, yellow patches of desert, blue swirls of ocean, green swatches of rain forest, dark gray lines of **MOUNTAIN RANGES**, and the SPARKLING silver snow of polar ice caps. It was an incredible sight.

All around them was the dense **BLACK** of the universe! As the *Starcruise* sped away,

it seemed as though Earth was escaping, floating far off, getting smaller and smaller and shining more and more BRIGHTLY.

"The atmosphere is so delicate . . . like a silk veil!" whispered Paulina, her squeak trembling with excitement.

Colette's eyes were bright with emotion. "It's the most beautiful thing I've ever seen!"

Floundering through the air, Pamela and Nicky finally reached their friends. "Come fly with us!" they urged them.

When they saw what the others were looking at, Pam's snout dropped open with wonder, and Nicky took out the camera she had brought to commemorate the moment.

FROM THE EARTH TO THE MOON!

It took four days to fly to the moon. The THEA SISTERS and Napoleon Smith passed the time by admiring the wonders of the universe around them. It was all so amazing the mouselets wanted to soak in every moment.

The **enthusiasm** of their fellow travelers, on the other paw, wore off QUICKLY. Despite the extensive training they had done underwater, it was very difficult to control movement.

Everyone always ended up bumping into something or someone else.

THUMP...

BOOM

OOMPH!

OUCH!

SORRY!

HEY, LOOK WHERE YOU'RE FLYING!

That was more or less the sound track of the trip!

Greta Van Rodenten scoffed at the quality

SPACE FOOD

During space voyages, food is freeze-dried. Then, just before it's time to eat, the food is put in a "**rehydration station**." This device puts just enough water back into the food and then heats it up. Freeze-dried foods are kept in special containers, which must be opened with care so the food doesn't float away!

of the FOOD they were served, even though it had been prepared by a renowned French chef.

As for Ricky Newsmouse, he liked the food a little *too* much, a fact that Ian Focus was happy to point out. "You're going to get sick, just like that time you barfed in the middle of the Amazon RAIN FOREST."

"Oh, quit your COMPLAINING! Good food inspires my writing!" replied Ricky, popping a cheese puff into his mouth and swallowing it with one big CHOMP. "I've already written three articles. I bet

ADAPTING TO SPACE

The absence of gravity on the moon can have a negative physical impact on astronauts. Without gravity, bones and muscles start to grow weaker. That's why astronauts need to exercise at least **two hours a day** to keep in shape.

Furthermore, in a space shuttle or a space station, there is no up or down. This, too, can create problems for the astronauts until they get used to their strange new environment.

Newsmouse was sitting on the ceiling! For him it seemed natural enough, but when he looked at Focus, it appeared as though his partner was pedaling with his snout facing downward!

you can't say the same about your famouse photos!"

The three investors continued with their calculations, filling out **CHARTS** and GRAPHS and **pepperinng** Napoleon Smith with questions. They wanted to know everything about the **CONSTRUCTION** of the spacecraft.

On the fourth day, as planned, the *Starcruise* went into orbit around the moon. Napoleon Smith gathered everyone together and announced seriously: "Friends, the moment has arrived!

In a minute, we will set paw on the moon!"

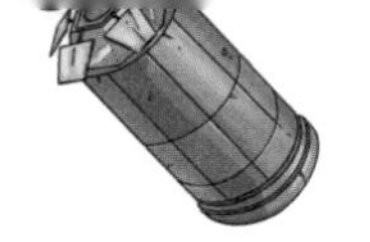

WE'RE LANDING ON THE MOON!

Smith's words had a ***mind-blowing*** effect on the travelers (and also a pretty funny effect, just as he'd hoped!).

"**WHAAAAAAT?!?**" shrieked Greta Van Rodenten. She **LEAPED** from her seat and hit her **snout** on the ceiling. "Ouch!"

As Focus came to her rescue, Newsmouse exclaimed, "No one told us we would be setting **PAW** on the moon! I thought we were just going around it!"

"Oh, no, we can't. It's not in the budget!" PROTESTED the three investors, flipping through their notes feverishly. "This has not been calculated into the COSTS!"

"I thought everyone would enjoy this special SURPRISE," Napoleon told the group. "If you look outside, in a bit you will be able to see it with your own EYES."

Nicky and Pamela already had their snouts SQUISHED against the window. "I can't

see anything! It's all **black**," Nicky said.

"We are circling **behind** the moon," explained Napoleon. "It will just take another minute, and then we'll see the DARK side, the part you can't see from Earth. . . ."

THE DARK SIDE OF THE MOON

The moon spins on its axis while it circles Earth. For this reason, the moon always shows Earth the same side, and we never see the other. The side of the moon we don't see is called the **dark side**, because it's hidden!

Violet JUMPED up and pointed to a spot far below them on the moon's surface. "There are lights down there!"

"Ladies and gentlemice, may I present . . . TITANIA!" Mr. Smith declared.

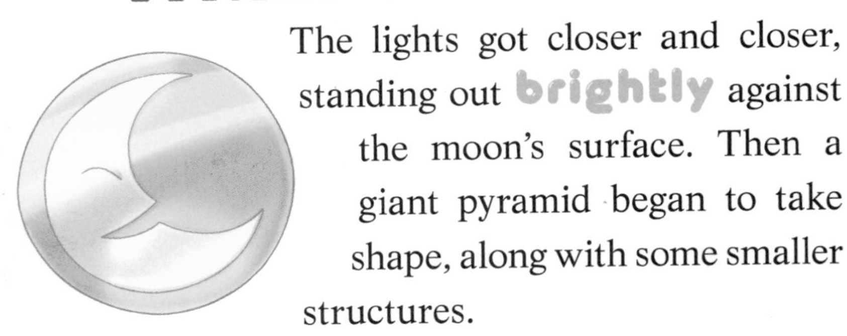

The lights got closer and closer, standing out brightly against the moon's surface. Then a giant pyramid began to take shape, along with some smaller structures.

"It looks like the pyramid at the preparation base, only bigger!" Nicky **OBSERVED**.

"Well, don't keep us licking our whiskers in SUSPENSE, Smith!" said Greta. "Tell us what it is!"

Napoleon proudly **puffed** up his fur. "TITANIA is the first and only resort village on the moon!"

"So should we prepare for the *Starcruise* to land?" asked Focus.

"No, UNFORTUNATELY!" Napoleon answered. "The landing pad isn't ready for such large vehicles."

"So just how are we supposed to GET DOWN there? Flap our paws and fly like birds?" interrupted Greta ACIDLY.

"We have two small service crafts aboard this shuttle. We will use those," Napoleon responded calmly. "If you're not feeling up to the challenge, you are more than welcome to stay here. But of course, then you won't have much of a tale to tell when you return to EARTH!"

Greta fell silent: No journalist worth her cheese would turn down the chance for a SCOOP like that!

MOON LANDING

Before scampering aboard the two service crafts, everyone had to put on their heavy, pressurized **space suits**. Greta found dozens of reasons to complain. She MOANED and WHINED so much that Napoleon Smith decided she should depart on the first service craft, along with Professor Golden, Newsmouse, Focus, and the investors. Napoleon Smith and the THEA SISTERS would follow on the second one.

But Greta wouldn't hear of it. "I won't be

Astronauts land on the moon in a special part of the spaceship called the **lunar module**, which is separate from the main body of the ship. The *Apollo 11* mission was the first to take human beings to the moon. *Apollo 11*'s lunar module, called *Eagle*, separated from the spacecraft and landed in an area of the moon called the Sea of Tranquility.

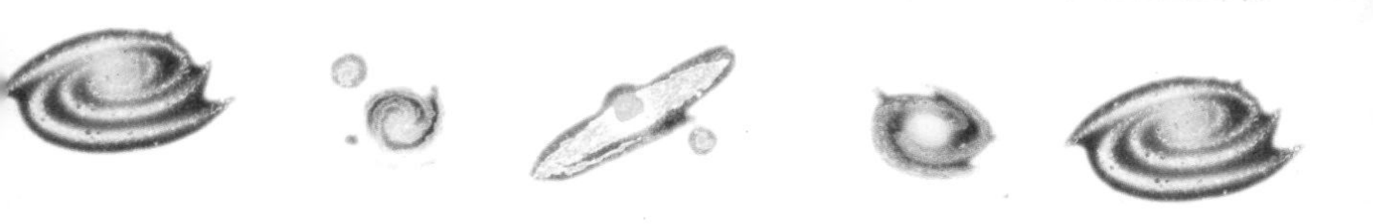

the first to go!" she cried, stomping her paw. Then she waved a paw at the investors. "And I absolutely **REFUSE** to travel with those three. Their constant calculations are giving me a **HEADACHE**!"

Violet turned to Napoleon and said, "I'll take her place on the first craft, if that's okay with you, Mr. Smith."

"Why, Violet, you are more *gracious* than my great-aunt *Kindpaws*," he responded gratefully. "Let's make sure one of your friends goes with you."

So the inseparable THEA SISTERS were **DIVIDED**, right at the most important moment of their journey: the last leg toward the moon!

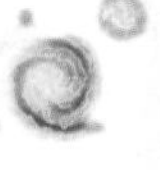

Paulina accompanied Violet, and they traded places with Greta Van Rodenten and Ian Focus. They realized they were playing

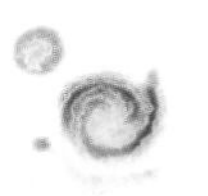

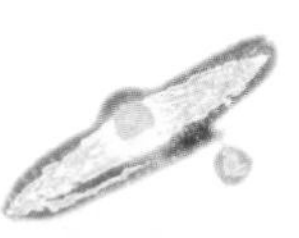

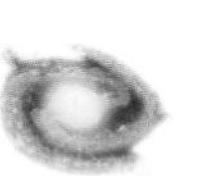

right into Greta's PAWS by separating Newsmouse from Focus, but Violet felt it was worth it to keep the peace.

The seven passengers took an elevator inside the *Starcruise* to the bay where the two service crafts were located. The small craft looked like circular towers with hexagonal domes on top. All seven rodents **climbed** into the dome of the first one and

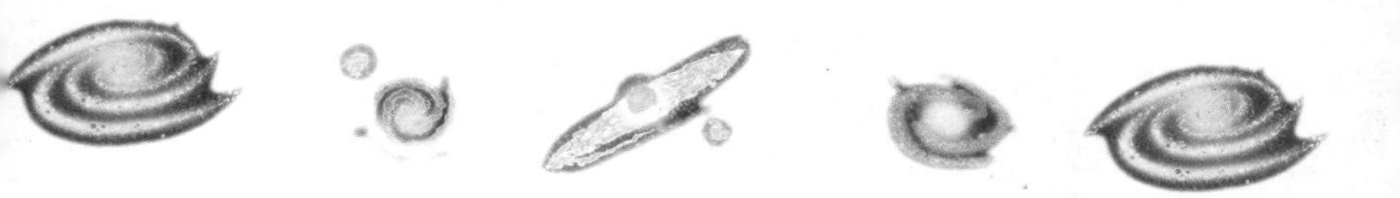

found a comfortable cabin for their short flight.

As the craft separated from the *Starcruise*, the mice felt a big jolt. Paulina and Violet looked at each other in alarm. But after that first bump, the trip to the moon was slow and peaceful. All around them, the universe seemed DARK and MYSTERIOUS, filled with gently shining stars.

Their landing on the moon's surface was so soft that it seemed to Paulina that the small spacecraft had landed on a cat-fur **mattress**.

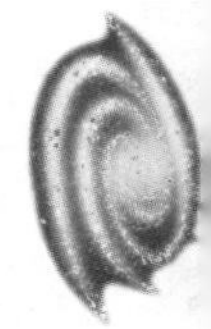

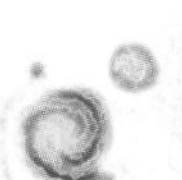

As the doors slid open, the passengers heard strains of music. A band of musical ROBOTS was there to greet them!

"Musical robots!" exclaimed Paulina in delight. "What will Mr. Smith think of next?"

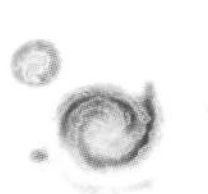

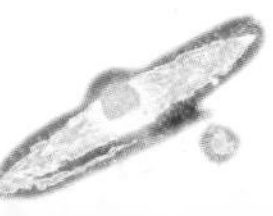

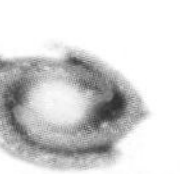

BANG! SPACEWRECK!

When the *Starcruise* got word that the first craft had arrived safely at Titania, the second one was allowed to **DEPART**. Mr. Smith, Colette, Nicky, Pam, Focus, and Greta made themselves comfortable. Since the first moon **LANDING** had gone so smoothly, everyone felt calm and relaxed. Until . . .

BANG!

A sudden noise shook the spacecraft, creating quite a fright among the passengers. Next came a series of small knocks, as if it were hailing outside.

BONK-BINK-BONK-PLUNK-PINK-PONK!

"**MOLDY MOON ROCKS, WHAT'S HAPPENING?!**" squeaked Greta in panic.

"It must be a meteor shower!" exclaimed Focus.

Pamela saw a **SCREW** flash past the window. "It's not meteors!" she cried. "It's a ***SWARM*** of space junk!"

Napoleon Smith was desperately trying to get in contact with the *Starcruise* when suddenly there was a much larger sound!

KA-BOOOM!

The tiny spacecraft shuddered and spun around. Then it began to fall toward the moon's surface!

SPACE JUNK

Space missions have created a large quantity of **space junk**, which circles Earth. Impact with this rubble can cause serious damage to satellites. To resolve the problem, experts from all over the world are trying to figure out rules to help guide the disposal of materials in space.

KA-BOOOM!

EEEEEEEEEEEEEEEEEEEEEEK!

Colette, Nicky, and Pam grabbed one another's paws for comfort and courage.

A moment later, they CRASHED onto the moon!

At TITANIA, Paulina and Violet were unaware of what was happening to their friends. They were busy *singing* one of Paulina's favorite Peruvian songs. The **robot** band was phenomenal! Mr. Smith's creations could play ROCK, **jazz**, and Argentine tango, and they even changed their looks to match the feel of each song. That's right: The robots were able to **change** shape and color according to the **rhythm**!

IT'S NOT JUST SCIENCE FICTION!

The **Haile** (pronounded Hi-lee) robot, created by a professor at Georgia Tech, knows how to play the drums. It can listen to what other musicians are playing and accompany them, adjusting the beat as necessary.

The same communicators they had used at the preparation base could be used with the robots at Titania, so Paulina had asked the band to **play** a song from her country.

Most of the passengers wanted to wait for the **arrival** of the second service craft in the moon-port's waiting room. But Professor Golden had **WANDERED** away for a

while, and when he returned, he said eagerly, "Let's go visit the **SPACE YARD**!"

"Shouldn't we wait for the others to get here?" asked Newsmouse.

Violet nodded. "You took the words right out of my mouth."

"Oh, I'm sure your friends are docking by now. There's no reason to wait! Besides, there isn't enough room for our whole party on the **Moon-o-rail**. Let's **LOOK AROUND** first, and they can do the same when they get here. **COME ON!**"

With that, the professor strode away. The others glanced at one another questioningly, then followed him.

Why is Professor Golden so anxious to leave before the others arrive?

ON THE MOON'S SURFACE

Napoleon, Nicky, Colette, Pamela, Focus, and Greta carefully scrambled out of the **FALLEN** service craft. They were all a little **dazed** as they climbed onto the moon's

surface. Thanks to the low gravity, they were tripping and bouncing with every pawstep.

Fortunately, no one was hurt. Their thick, resistant space suits had protected them. Also, the SANDY ground and the weak force of the moon's gravity had softened the impact.

Unfortunately, the spacecraft was no longer usable, the radio was broken, and they were thirty-five miles from Titania! "And that's give or take a mile," added Napoleon, discouraged, as he gazed at the detailed moon map on his foldable screen.

Greta was exasperated. "Well, hurry up and call for help, then! We can't scurry all that way on PAW!"

"That would be unthinkable!" agreed Focus, examining the **GROUND**. "We can barely control our movements in this low **gravity**!"

Napoleon tried to stay **POSITIVE**. "The radio isn't **working**, but the *Starcruise* certainly must have alerted Professor Golden at **TITANIA**! Nonetheless, it could take them a while to find us. I propose we use the Moon Rover."

"**Moon Rover?** What's that?" asked Pamela hopefully. "Some kind of SUV for the moon?" She loved anything with wheels.

Napoleon nodded. "Something like that, yes. It's a vehicle that we use to move across the moon's surface. I hope it's not **broken**."

"If it is, no problem!" Nicky piped up. "Pam is a fabumouse mechanic. In fact, you might even say she's **out of this world**!"

Napoleon smiled at the mouselets' trust in and enthusiasm for one another, even at that DIFFICULT moment. Then he turned to Focus. "Ian, can you please help me pull the Moon Rover out of the service craft?"

The Moon Rover didn't seem to have been damaged in the crash. It started up immediately. Even though it wasn't exactly the prettiest vehicle, Pamela was dying to drive it. But she didn't have the COURAGE to ask Napoleon, who had seated himself at the wheel.

"Uh, what's that?" asked Pam, pointing to one of the many gadgets on the dashboard. "It looks like a radio! Can't we use it?"

"OF COURSE! It's a two-way

radio," explained Napoleon. "All lunar vehicles come equipped with radios. How could I have forgotten?"

But no matter how many times they tried to reach Titania, they got no answer.

"The radio must be DAMAGED," Napoleon concluded in disappointment.

"Well, let's not waste any more time," Colette said. "LET'S GO!"

Mr. Smith started the engine, and the vehicle stuttered to life and began rumbling along the rough lunar surface.

Rumble Rumble Rumble

Unfortunately, the Moon Rover was slower than a fat RAT after a seven-cheese meal!

The Moon Rover's radio is broken, too. What a series of unfortunate coincidences!

ONE GIANT LEAP FOR MOUSEKIND

Meanwhile, the other group of astromice scurried **quickly** to the streets of Titania. They climbed on board the **Moon-o-rail**, a vehicle with a ***FUTURISTIC*** design that glided along a metal strip. They hadn't the

slightest idea that their companions were in TROUBLE!

Professor Golden was their guide through the vast space yard, where the robots were able to work even in darkness. Since they operated during both the day and night, construction was progressing swiftly. "This is the sports area. The pools and the covered gymnasiums are almost complete. And we will also build a stadium for games that are suited to the moon's low gravity."

All the workers were robots, but each one was programmed to complete a different task. At that moment, the space yard was lit up as if it were daylight. Rows of light boards gave off a pinkish light that was relaxing and quite pleasant.

"Is it always nighttime here?" asked Mr. Watermouse, perplexed.

"This lighting system must cost a FORTUNE!" commented an alarmed Mr. Hooper.

"How much electricity do the robots use?" Mr. Rice asked. He looked worried.

For a split second, Professor Golden's serious snout contained a hint of a smile. "The robots produce their own energy, and that is all they need to function. They get it from the regolith, which is a type of SAND that covers the moon. As for the lighting . . ."

Professor Golden stopped the Moon-o-rail next to one of the light boards. "LOOK

IT'S NOT JUST SCIENCE FICTION!

The moon's surface is covered by a layer of dust and rubble called **regolith**. Regolith is rich with hydrogen, an element that is being studied for possible use as an energy source—as fuel for rockets, for example.

IT'S NOT JUST SCIENCE FICTION!

Scientists are working on a new way of creating electric light. Instead of coming from bulbs, it could be emitted directly from house walls, furniture, and even pillows!

closely! There are no bulbs. The material itself lights up. All the buildings in Titania are equipped with walls like this."

Ricky Newsmouse was filming everything with his video camera. "Why, it's fantastic!" he exclaimed. "It's like living in the future!"

"But is it really always night here?" asked Mr. Watermouse. He didn't know much about the moon.

Violet answered him. "One day on the moon is about twenty-nine days on Earth. This means that based on Earth's time, on the moon we alternate . . . let's see here . . . fourteen and a half days of **light** and the same amount of **DARKNESS**!*"

* Take a look at the chart of the lunar phases on page 11, and you'll see that Violet is correct.

Finally, the group finished its tour of the **resort** village and reached the hotel. Only then did everyone **realize** that the second service craft had not arrived.

AT THE BOTTOM OF A CRATER

Meanwhile, the Moon Rover was gradually making its way up and down the rocky lunar surface.

Rumble Rumble Rumble

"Traveling in this bucket of **BOLTS** is slower than riding on a turtle's back! We might as well have waited where we crashed," Greta moaned.

For once, the others couldn't disagree.

"The Moon Rover doesn't go any faster than this," explained Mr. Smith apologetically.

"Can I take a look at the motor?" asked Pam. "Maybe something was damaged during the **CRASH**."

So Pamela got to work, although it wasn't easy with her bulky **SPACE SUIT** and gloves on! The wrench kept slipping from her grasp, and the **SCREWS** started floating away. Focus offered to be her assistant; he seemed to know his way around motors.

After half an hour of tinkering, they found a few things that were out of place, and Pam was able to **FIX** them. Then she tried to restart the Moon Rover, and . . .

VROOM-VROOM-VROOOMMMMM!!

"That's much better!" Pam exclaimed with satisfaction. Then she added **hopefully**, "Can I drive this time?"

Napoleon happily surrendered the wheel to her. "Sure! You've earned it. You really know your way around a motor!"

Pamela sat down and put her **PAW** on

the gas. "Now we'll cover those thirty-five miles in a **flash**!"

Unfortunately, she quickly discovered that the moon is not meant to be crossed at high **SPEEDS**. Between the **ROCKY** terrain, the craters, and the low gravity, the moon's surface was more treacherous than the New Mouse City **freeway** at rush hour.

When Pam picked up speed, the passengers almost ended up in **orbit**! The **vehicle** reared upward and skidded up a **STEEP HILL** as if it were a takeoff ramp. After a **FLIGHT** of a couple hundred feet, the vehicle landed right at the edge of another steep **SLOPE**.

"Brake, Pam, brake!" urged Nicky.

"I am **BRAKING**!" yelled her friend, leaning on the brakes with all her **weight**.

But it didn't matter. The

Moon Rover wasn't responding! It slipped down . . . farther and farther down . . . **UNTIL IT LANDED AT THE BOTTOM OF A CRATER**!

PRISONERS OF TITANIA

Back at TITANIA, Professor Golden kept trying to reach the second service craft.

"They're not answering!" he said, hanging up the receiver.

"Call the *Starcruise*, then!" responded Ricky Newsmouse, worried.

But the professor shook his snout. "That's not possible right now! It's *flying* around the moon. It's beyond the satellite's reach,

and it will be a while before we can get in contact with their radio."

PAULINA couldn't believe her ears. "We can't just wait around and not do ANYTHING! Something must have happened!" she burst out.

The professor answered her calmly. In fact, he squeaked quite slowly, as though to a tiny mouseling: "The *Starcruise* has a built-in warning system. If something had happened to the service craft, I would have been notified! But there's been no word."

"But our friends haven't arrived!" replied

Paulina. Her snout had turned red with frustration.

"Well, maybe they never left!" snapped the professor.

"Or maybe they had to make an EMERGENCY landing!" Violet countered.

"If that's the case, they should still be able to contact us," Professor Golden replied **SHARPLY**. "They'd have the Moon Rover, a lunar vehicle equipped with a two-way radio."

Violet maintained her calm, but she had no intention of giving up. "Well, we should at least take a *patrol* ride, to make sure nothing's happened."

Newsmouse nodded. "She's right! I saw some vehicles in the storage depot. Let's get them and check out the area!"

"**ABSOLUTELY NOT!**" declared

Professor Golden. "The Moon Rovers are not to be touched. I strictly prohibit anyone from leaving TITANIA!" With that, he called three robots and ordered them to stand guard in front of the exit GATES.

Once the robots had obeyed, he turned back to the little group. "I am responsible for your safety, and I intend to get you all back to Earth safe and sound! Now, please, go and rest in your rooms. We are all very TIRED."

Mr. Rice, Mr. Watermouse, and Mr. Hooper obeyed the professor's ORDERS without hesitation. But Paulina and Violet were reluctant to follow them. The two FRIENDS were way too worried to sleep!

Paulina and Violet exchanged glances.

Professor Golden insists there's no need to search, but is he sincere when he says that there's nothing to worry about?

Paulina pointed one paw to a service exit nearby. Violet nodded.

A moment later, the two mouselets snuck into the storage depot. They had just stepped into the poorly lit room when a voice hissed, "Who's there?"

Violet almost JUMPED out of her fur. "Mr. Newsmouse!?!" she exclaimed. She was surprised and relieved at the same time. "What are you doing here?"

"The same thing you're doing: disobeying ORDERS!" Newsmouse responded with a laugh.

"Well, we certainly can't go to bed when our friends could be in DANGER out there!" declared Paulina. She was still furious at the professor for not listening to their concerns.

The expression on the journalist's snout softened. "You are DETERMINED and COURAGEOUS," he said. "You remind me of my partner and me at your age. I can't count the number of times Ian saved me from trouble. . . ." His squeak trailed off. "Well, that's enough of that little trip down memory lane. Come on, let's get to work! Do you have any idea how to start a Moon Rover?"

"Well, we don't have the KEYS to the ignition," Paulina replied in surprise.

"That's true. But I don't see a keyhole, anyway," noted Newsmouse.

Violet stroked her fur thoughtfully. "Grandpa Chen always said, 'Gentleness is the MASTER KEY that opens all doors!' Maybe our communicators will work." She touched the communicator and said, "Please OPEN the door, Moon Rover!"

At once, the door of the Moon Rover swung open.

"WOW! It works!" Paulina rejoiced, hopping in. As soon as Violet and Newsmouse were settled in, she squeaked into her communicator, "Now, Moon Rover, start your engine!"

VRROOOOOMMMM!!!

"Good work!" exclaimed Newsmouse. "Now all that's left to do is learn how to DRIVE it."

"Mr. Newsmouse, why don't you try to figure out what all these buttons on the dashboard do?" said Violet. "Paulina and I will try to get the robots away from the gate."

ROBOT VS. ROBOT!

Paulina and Violet scampered over to the nearest gate. A TALL robot was standing in front of it.

When Violet politely asked him if they could pass, he responded sternly: "First order: No one can leave!"

Violet and Paulina nodded and retreated a few feet.

PAULINA was struck by his words. "The **ROBOT** considers what the professor said to be a '*first order*,' and we can't cancel it with just our communicators,"

she mused. She thought for a moment or two; then she gave up. "Does your grandfather have any suggestions about STUBBORN robots?" she asked Violet.

Violet smiled. "Well . . . there was this one time when I didn't want to go to a party with my mother. Grandpa Chen told me, 'If you and another rodent can't agree about something, change the SUBJECT!'"

She pointed to the robot and added, "We don't know how smart these robots are. So let's trying changing the subject! What do you say we try to distract him?"

Paulina's snout lit up. "That's it! I know just how to do it!" She took Violet by the PAW and led her back into the storage depot. "Let's see if Mr. Newsmouse has learned how to drive the Moon Rover . . . then we'll start the music!"

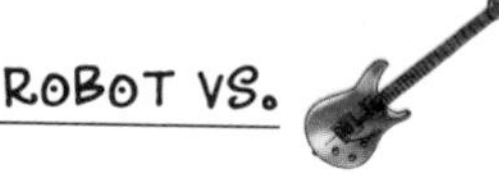

Violet was confused. "Music?!? What do you mean, music?"

Paulina grinned. "We'll use the robot musicians to keep the GUARD away!"

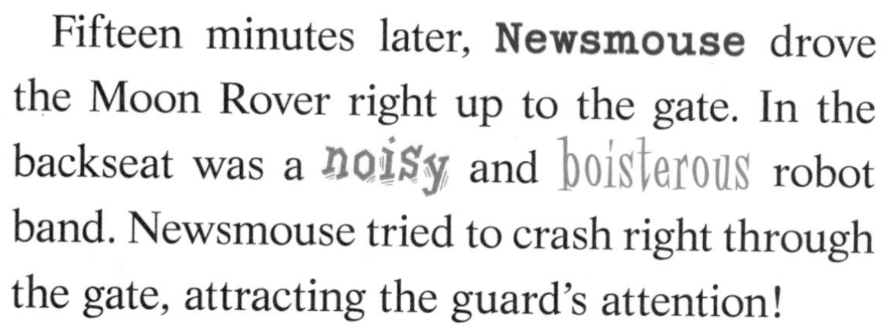

Fifteen minutes later, **Newsmouse** drove the Moon Rover right up to the gate. In the backseat was a noisy and boisterous robot band. Newsmouse tried to crash right through the gate, attracting the guard's attention!

Just as Violet had predicted, the guard's intelligence wasn't very *sophisticated*. Forgetting the orders to keep watch over the gate, the guard followed Newsmouse's Moon Rover as it drove away.

Newsmouse quickly JAMMED the accelerator and jumped out of the vehicle, letting the **robots** fight it out among

themselves. Then he caught up to a second Moon Rover, where the two THEA SISTERS were waiting for him. As soon as he was safe on board, Violet pronounced the magic words: "Open the gate!"

The gate slowly swung open. They were FREE!

Paulina looked at the DASHBOARD of the Moon Rover with fascination; it was covered with gadgets. One of them looked like a radio! She quickly switched it on. On the display appeared a list of possibilities, one of which was OFF BASE: MAX 300 MILES.

"Maybe this is a way to communicate with vehicles that are outside the base!" Paulina cried. She touched the display, and the radio began to send out A SIGNAL.

BEEP BEEP BEEP BEEP BEEP BEEP BEEP BEEP BEEP

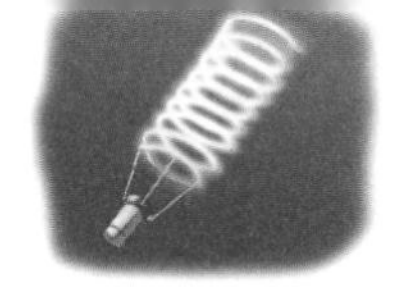

CLOSER FRIENDS THAN EVER BEFORE!

Meanwhile, five of the six **moon wreck** survivors were **PUSHING** their **Moon Rover** out of the crater. The low **gravity** worked in their favor. If they had been on Earth, their situation would have been impossible. On the moon, however, it was just really, really hard!

"**UPPHHH!**" snorted Colette when they stopped to catch their **breath** halfway up.

"Just a little bit more, LAZYFUR!" said Nicky affectionately. "You don't want to be like that WHINER Greta, do you? She just SITS there watching everyone else do the heavy lifting!"

Colette LOOKED UP at the journalist, who was sitting alone at the top of the crater, enjoying the view. Colette's whiskers trembled with fury. "Let's give it all we've got! We're nearly there!" she shouted.

When they finally got the Moon Rover out of the crater, Mr. Smith and Pamela sat down and sighed with relief. The others joined them.

Colette looked around at the horizon. She saw Earth in the distance, and her eyes filled with TEARS. Then, looking a little closer, she noticed a WHITISH cloud of dust moving toward them.

"There's a vehicle **DOWN THERE**!" she yelled. "They're coming to get us!"

At that instant, the Moon Rover's radio began beeping.

CLUE!

BEEP BEEP BEEP BEEP BEEP BEEP

Focus raced to the receiver and picked it up. "**HELLO?! HELLO?!**" he shouted. "**HELLO? CAN YOU HEAR ME?!**"

"**HA! HA! HA!**" A familiar laugh answered his question.

"Is that really you, you SPINELESS old sewer rat?" asked Focus, bursting with joy.

"How are you, you **brainless** pack rat?" Newsmouse replied. His words were fierce, but his squeak was trembling with **emotion**.

"We're all right, but our service craft crashed and the Moon Rover ended up in a crater!" Focus replied.

The Moon Rover's radio works! Why didn't anyone answer when Napoleon first called? (Look at the clue on page 84!)

"Are Colette, Nicky, and Pamela with you?" Paulina's squeak cut in ANXIOUSLY.

"Yes, we're here, and we're FINE, Paulina!" yelled Pam. "We just made it out of the crater when Colette spotted someone coming!"

"It's us!" exclaimed Violet HAPPILY. "We see you!"

Newsmouse, Paulina, and Violet had indeed caught sight of some small lights flickering in the distance. They SPED UP to reach their friends, but after Pam warned

them of the dangers of going too fast, they kept a reasonable pace so they wouldn't end up in a **CRATER** like their friends had!

A few minutes later, the two groups were TOGETHER again. The THEA SISTERS threw their paws around one another, and Newsmouse and Focus did the same. Napoleon Smith gave everyone **HUGS** all around.

As Newsmouse was **GREETING** his friend, he thought of the fear he'd felt when Focus was in danger. It put the disputes between him and his partner in perspective. He gazed at the THEA SISTERS, who were smiling and holding one another's paws. *Their friendship and their enthusiasm for the mission is still intact,* he thought. *Maybe Ian and I can be like that again . . . maybe it's not too late for us to rediscover the partnership we had when we were* ***mouselets****!*

As if Focus had read his mind, he looked Newsmouse square in the **EYES** and said, "You know what, Ricky? We're too old and **WISE** to spend all our time **ARGUING** like a couple of **SEWER RATS** fighting over a piece of **SWISS**! From now on, let's try harder to sort things out. If we work at it, we can be closer friends than ever before."

Newsmouse **smiled** and grabbed his old friend's paw.

As for Greta, she stood awkwardly next to the **Moon Rover**. She was **disappointed**: She'd done her best to separate Newsmouse and Focus, but now they seemed **closer** than ever!

RETURN TO TITANIA

Naturally, the six SPACEWRECK survivors were exhausted from their adventure. So it was a delight to arrive at TITANIA and be greeted by the robot band and their happy welcome music.

Professor Golden apologized at once. He seemed very UPSET with himself for not having rushed to help them. And he praised Newsmouse, Violet, and Paulina, dubbing them "the most intrepid rodent RESCUE squad in all of SPACE."

"You acted *wisely*, Sebastian," Napoleon said, consoling him, being generous, as always. "You were responsible for all the guests, and you were only thinking about the safety of the group."

The THEA SISTERS didn't agree, but they kept quiet as mice: They were too happy to spoil the moment!

Greta, on the other paw, was chewing her whiskers. "This trip stinks worse than rotten cheese! Just wait until I tell all my television viewers!"

That was quite a blow to Napoleon. FORTUNATELY, Newsmouse and Focus intervened.

"Oh, stop it, Greta! Accidents can happen!" said Focus.

"Titania is fabumouse!" insisted Newsmouse. "All the technology is super-advanced! It's like living in a science fiction movie!"

"Hrmph! I think it's more like living at the top of COLDCREEPS PEAK! *BRRR!*" Greta replied, shivering.

By then, everyone had taken off their

space suits. It was a little chilly in the hotel.

"Oh, I'll soon fix that," Napoleon assured them. "How about a dip in a nice, warm Jacuzzi? After that, I promise you a whisker-licking good lunch!"

A robot led the THEA SISTERS to their suite.

"Leaping lunar lemmings!" exclaimed Pamela as they entered the suite's living room.

"What a dream!" Colette agreed.

"I can hardly believe my eyes," whispered Paulina, breathless with disbelief.

The room was ENORMOUSE, with a gorgeous mosaic floor, large off-white couches that looked extra-soft, and walls that emitted a glowing light. But the mouselets hardly noticed any of that. They looked toward the sky as if they were

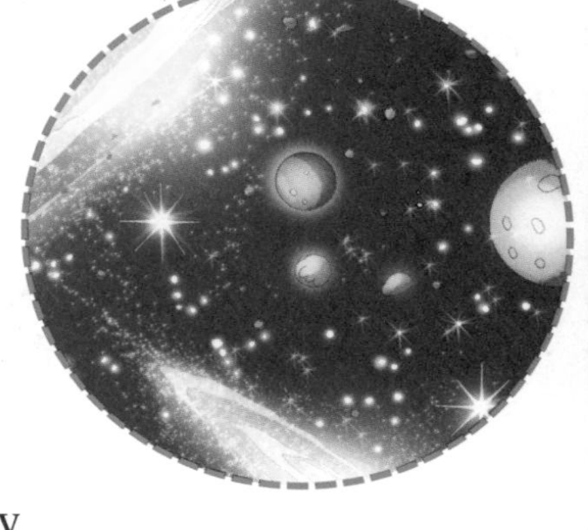

hypnotized: They could see the entire starry universe through the glass ceiling!

Colette, Nicky, Pamela, Paulina, and Violet immediately dropped their luggage and threw themselves onto the couches, keeping their snouts turned up toward the heavens. They lay there in silence, overwhelmed by all the beauty.

After a few minutes, Colette realized that she was sitting in a pool of sweat. "Is it just me, or is it hotter than fondue in a pot in here?"

"You're right!" said Pamela. "First it was too cold, and now it's the opposite!"

First it was too cold; now it's too hot! Why is all this sophisticated electronic equipment misbehaving?

A ROBOT REVOLT!

Colette touched her communicator and called a **robot** to their suite. "Please adjust the thermostat. It's too **HOT** in our suite!"

The robot came in and reached for what looked like a **PAINTING**. At the robot's touch, the beautiful painted **LANDSCAPE** vanished, and thermometers appeared on the **GLASS** panel. All of them were showing very **high** temperatures.

Paulina nodded in relief. "Great!" she said. "Now the robot can adjust it. . . ."

But her squeak trailed off as the **robot** pulled a **HAMMER** out of a compartment and started slamming it into the control panel.

CRAAASH!

"*Aaaaaargh!*" shrieked the mouselets. They fled their suite and headed to the lobby. Once they got there, they discovered that their **robots** weren't the only ones that had malfunctioned. **Chaos** had erupted throughout the hotel. All of the **robots** were **OUT OF CONTROL**. The once silent and efficient mechanical staff had become hostile, touchy, and **rude**!

Everyone gathered in the hotel lobby to gripe about the **robots**. The only mice

CLUE!

missing were Ricky Newsmouse and Ian Focus. Mr. Rice told the THEA SISTERS that he had asked for some **tea**, and his robot served him a **cream cheese** pie . . . right in his **snout**! Mr. Watermouse had been in the **Bath** when a robot decided to dump a can of **SPACE JUNK** in with him. And Mr. Hooper had watched in horror as a robot took a wrench to his precious **calculator** and gave it an unwanted upgrade.

Even the members of the **robot** band, who had been such great musicians, were now deliberately making **ear-shattering**, tail-twisting sounds!

"This place is worse than a week at Lousy Leopard Lodge!" cried Greta Van Rodenten. "**I WANT TO GO HOME!**"

The three businessmice turned red with **RAGE**. "Titania is a **FAILURE**! The risks are sky-high! And there's no hope of making a **profit**!"

Napoleon Smith refused to give up. He tried to **calm** everyone down. "This is just an unfortunate accident! Professor Golden is trying to find a solution."

At that moment, an **ENORMOUSE** robot burst into the lobby, carrying Newsmouse and Focus by their **tails**.

All the robots seem to be malfunctioning! Could it be just another incredible coincidence?

THE USUAL SUSPECTS . . .

Napoleon calmed everyone down and asked them to return to their suites until he came up with a **plan**. The **THEA SISTERS** tried to pull themselves together after the **SCARE**.

"What a **NIGHTMARE**!" commented Pamela as soon as they'd closed their door. "Of course, **accidents** can always happen, like Focus said, but things seem to be

GOING DOWNHILL FAST!"

Colette nodded. "I hate to agree with Greta, but Titania is a real DISASTER!"

"And yet, when we took that ride around the grounds, everything was WORKING perfectly," Paulina mused. "It's strange that everything changed so *suddenly*!"

Violet, who had been silent until then, squeaked up: "An accident is nothing more than a matter of chance. Two accidents are a case of coincidence or bad luck. But three accidents . . . that seems like a plan!"

"Wait, do you mean sabotage?" asked Pamela, astounded.

Violet nodded. "Something's **afoot**, and it's not at the end of my **leg**. Think about it, mouselings. When you combine what's happened with Professor Golden's strange behavior . . ."

"Yeah, there is something that doesn't **add up**!" agreed Paulina. "The second service craft crashes, and he doesn't know anything about it."

"And the radio onboard just happened to be **broken**," Nicky added.

"Why didn't the *Starcruise* tell Professor Golden about the accident before the radio transmissions were **interrupted**? He is the director of this whole project!" Paulina wondered. "Even the radio on the **Moon Rover** seemed to be broken, but when I called, Focus responded **immediately**. Professor Golden, on the other paw, said there was no signal!"

Violet nodded again, more emphatically this time.

"And he's been so unfriendly! That's what makes me suspicious. He FORBADE us to leave the base and go looking for you!"

Colette STARED from one of her friends to the other, dismayed. "So you're saying that the scientist who created Titania with Mr. Smith is trying to undermine the entire project?"

"IMPOSSIBLE!" exclaimed Pam and Nicky together.

"It doesn't seem to make any sense," Violet admitted. "Plus, Mr. Smith trusts the professor completely, and he certainly knows him better than we do."

Paulina shrugged. "Maybe we're just letting our imaginations scamper away with us."

KNOCK, KNOCK, KNOCK!

At that moment, there was a loud rap at the door.

Colette peered through the peephole, then opened the door cautiously. Ricky Newsmouse and Ian Focus slipped into the room. Ian looked over his shoulder, as if to make sure no one was WATCHING them.

The two journalists had something very interesting to show the THEA SISTERS. "After everything that's happened, you're the only ones we can trust completely," Newsmouse explained.

"I was FILMING some images of the hotel when we noticed that Professor Golden was messing around with the robots," he said. "But when a robot noticed my video camera, it ripped it out of my paws and smashed it!"

"Oh, no!" said Nicky. "They don't want us to film what happens on the base."

"But the **robot** didn't notice I was taking pictures, too," added Focus, showing them a tiny digital camera. "Take a look at this."

The **mouselets** huddled around Focus's camera. On the screen, they could CLEARLY see the professor in front of a **robot**, removing a **BLUE** chip from its control panel.

Focus pressed a BUTTON on the camera's back and revealed another photograph, taken a few seconds later. This time, Professor Golden was inserting a **RED** chip into the robot.

"Moldy mozzarella!" exclaimed Violet, ASTONISHED.

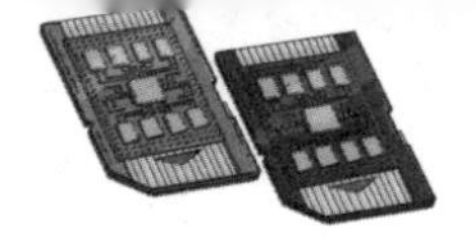

PREPARE FOR IMMEDIATE DEPARTURE!

Ian Focus showed the mouselets ENLARGED images of the BLUE and RED chips. "They look like memory cards, don't they?"

"It's **true**," agreed Paulina. "Maybe Professor Golden was trying to adjust them—"

"Or *break them*!" Focus interrupted. "Before the professor changed that robot's card, all the robots were behaving normally. Right after that, they attacked us!"

"**Violet**, it's starting to look more and more like your suspicions are correct," said Nicky.

"It looks like Professor Golden was able to affect all the **robots** by changing their

BLUE CHIP = positive responses from the robots

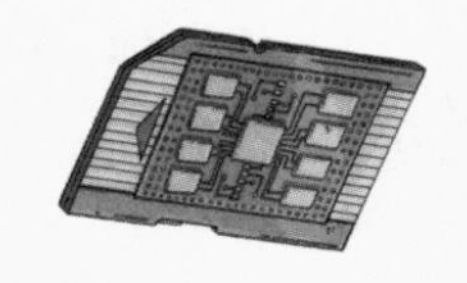

RED CHIP = negative responses from the robots

CHIPS." Paulina added. "Professor Golden programmed the robots to turn on the guests!"

"What a STINKY sewer rat!" snarled Focus. His snout had turned red with anger.

"But why?" asked Colette. She just couldn't understand the professor's behavior. "Why would he sabotage a project he's been working on for years?"

"Let's investigate his motives later," responded Newsmouse. "Right now, we need to figure out how to stop him. If he's the one who made the second service craft crash, something much worse could happen on board the *Starcruise* when we return!"

Paulina nodded thoughtfully. "Let's get the correct memory chips back into the robots," she said. "The BLUE ones, I mean. That's the only way we can restore ORDER."

"But how will we find the blue chips?" asked Nicky. "Professor Golden must have HIDDEN them."

"Don't you worry about that. I'll get it out of him. I'll teach that rat a lesson if it's the last thing I do!" declared Newsmouse.

The sound of a WAILING SIREN made them almost jump out of their fur. As soon as the alarm ended, Napoleon Smith's voice echoed from the loudsqueaker. "Everyone report to my study immediately! We must abandon the base! I **REPEAT**: WE MUST ABANDON THE BASE!"

The mouselets, Newsmouse, and Focus rushed to the study. When the entire group of astromice had assembled, Napoleon Smith turned to them with a distraught expression. "My friends, I want to extend my **sincerest** apologies! Professor Golden has just told me that a major malfunction has rendered the robots unpredictable and **DANGEROUS**. I have contacted the *Starcruise* so we may depart IMMEDIATELY!"

As Mr. Smith squeaked, his snout grew pale. His eyes, usually so *friendly*, filled with tears.

"When do we need to put our suits back on?" Paulina asked.

"Immediately!" responded Napoleon.

"Unfortunately, we only have one working service craft, so we will have to take two **TRIPS**."

"Who will leave first?" asked Greta eagerly. It was clear she wanted **OFF** the base as soon as possible.

"You, Professor Golden, and the THEA SISTERS," Napoleon replied. He looked **EXHAUSTED**.

Newsmouse ushered the Thea Sisters toward the door. "After you, **intrepid** mouselets!"

LIKE A BALLOON AT MOUSY'S THANKSGIVING DAY PARADE!

The decision to abandon TITANIA caught the Thea Sisters by surprise. "We are at the mercy of that RASCALLY rat Golden! And we can't do anything to expose him!" Paulina muttered to her FRIENDS.

Violet whispered back, "I don't think he'll hurt us while we're with him on the service craft. But I'm afraid that something terrible will happen to the rodents left here with those robots he tampered with!"

Meanwhile, they had reached the changing room, where Professor Golden was waiting for them with their space suits. He was already fussing with one of the complicated garments. And that gave Paulina an **idea**!

Quicker than a cat with a ball of YARN, she grabbed the professor's unattended communicator and **whispered** orders to the spider-bots, who were waiting to **connect** the cables of the scientist's space suit.

Efficient as always, the tiny **robots** crawled up the pants of his space suit. Before the professor realized what was happening, they were already hard at work.

"What?! But I didn't tell you to . . ." Professor Golden squeaked shrilly as his suit began to **inflate**.

You see, Paulina had carefully studied the structure of the **PRESSURIZED** suits and had realized that **helium** was used to inflate them. Yes, that's right—the same gas that's used to blow up balloons!

IT'S NOT JUST SCIENCE FICTION!

Helium is an odorless and colorless gas that is completely nontoxic. It's mixed with other gases to be used with deep-water immersion equipment and astronaut equipment. By itself, it is often used to inflate blimps and balloons.

Obeying Paulina's orders, the mini-robots connected one of the suit's tubes to a helium canister. Professor Golden's suit inflated in a flash. He looked like a BALLOON in the annual Mousy's Thanksgiving Day Parade!

As he floated through the air, Professor Golden tried to RIP the spider-bots off him. "Help! Get me down!" he shouted.

"Up, up, and away!" Pamela whispered, giggling behind her paws.

Meanwhile, Nicky had taken advantage of the confusion by rummaging through the pockets of the professor's lab coat, which was hanging from a hook nearby. "Here they are! The robots' memory CHIPS!" she exclaimed, waving a pawful of bright BLUE plastic chips in the air.

"Why, you little THIEF!" shouted the professor. "Give those back immediately. They're mine!" He thrashed around in midair, trying to grab the chips, but his sudden, HERKY-JERKY movements just propelled him into a wall.

BONK! He hit the ceiling. BANG! He hit the floor. BOINK! He hit the opposite wall. KERBOINGGG!

The professor's shrieks echoed along the corridors. Everyone on the base came running.

Mr. Smith was startled. "MOON ROCKS! What are you doing up there, Sebastian?" he exclaimed as he watched the professor pirouette through the air.

The THEA SISTERS exchanged glances: The moment had arrived to make Professor Golden confess!

THE PROFESSOR'S CONFESSION

The mouselets were prepared to pressure the professor, but there was no need. He was so traumatized by his midair experience that he told the truth at once. The THEA SISTERS had shamed him into it!

"I'm the one behind most of the accidents!" he admitted furiously. "I was determined to SABOTAGE the *Starcruise*'s first trip. I wanted the investors and the public to be **scared** by the lack of security on the *Starcruise* and Titania. I wanted them to turn their **tails** on your dream, Napoleon. And I wanted your whole industrial empire to CRUMBLE like a house of cheese crackers!"

Napoleon Smith shook his snout in

disbelief. "But why, Sebastian? Why? This was our dream, and you were my friend! For ten years, you were my closest confidant. I trusted you more than anyone!"

"Oh, Napoleon, you silly CHIPMUNK!" Golden said scornfully. "I didn't want your friendship; I wanted your MONEY!"

"But if you wanted a raise, you just needed to tell me!" Napoleon replied in surprise.

"Oh, I didn't want the leftover crumbs of your *fortune*," responded the professor. "I wanted all of it! The whole cheese QUESADILLA! I wanted my name on the project! I would have constructed a new TITANIA,

one that was **all mine**, with money from your rivals!"

Napoleon was squeakless. He flopped down on a bench, looking **exhausted** and defeated. The revelation of his friend's betrayal was too much for him.

Pamela piped up. "So you were willing to risk our lives for greed? Crash for cash?"

"No, I had nothing to do with that!" the professor said vehemently, and he seemed sincere. "It really was space garbage that caused the service craft's accident. The construction work on Titania filled the moon's orbit with trash."

"I want to believe you, but admit it: You used the accident to help your plan," said Nicky.

A sneaky smile appeared on Golden's bony snout. "Well, I can't pass up an opportunity when it falls right into my PAWS. When the *Starcruise* alerted me to the accident, I turned off the radio and pretended it was broken. If it hadn't been for Newsmouse and your nosy little friends, it would've taken days to find TITANIA!

And that would've been the end of Napoleon Smith and his PRECIOUS space expeditions!"

The THEA SISTERS had heard enough. Paulina turned to her friends. "Let's get to work fixing those **robots**!"

"You don't plan on getting close enough to those **crazy creatures** to put the chips back in, do you?!" asked Colette in alarm.

"There is a general **CONTROL ROOM**," said Mr. Smith. "From there, you can communicate with all the **robots** on the base at the same time. We can try to deactivate them."

"Great," said Nicky. "That way, we won't run any RISKS. Where is this **CONTROL ROOM**?"

"I'll take you there," Mr. Smith responded, **getting up**.

"Okay!" said Pam, clapping. "Let's move those paws, mouselets!"

RELAX!

It took practically no time at all for the THEA SISTERS to reach the control room and reprogram the robots. Now that the danger had passed, and Professor Golden couldn't do any further **DAMAGE**, Napoleon Smith's guests were in no hurry to leave the moon. Even Greta was **eager** to explore the comforts of the hotel, especially the fantastic levitation *massage*!

The THEA SISTERS filmed the moon from every angle and took lots of notes for the reports they planned to write upon their return to **MOUSEFORD ACADEMY**.

Newsmouse and Focus had become **partners** once more. And they turned out to be terrible **pranksters**! Their favorite victims were Mr. Rice, Mr. Watermouse, and Mr. Hooper.

As for the three investors, they were still glued to their calculators. They were happily tallying up their future **gains**.

And Napoleon Smith? He distracted himself from the professor's betrayal by focusing on making his **dreams** a reality. "**TITANIA** will be more **fun** than

any amousement park!" he said. "But it will have more to offer, too. We'll do experiments to find new vaccines and to discover new ways of bringing **water** to the **DESERT**. It will be **fabumouse**!"

At the end of the week, the second **service craft** was **FIXED**. Everyone returned to the *Starcruise*. They were sad to leave the moon, but the **THEA SISTERS** were looking forward to getting back to **MOUSEFORD ACADEMY**.

A few days later, they **landed** back at the preparation base. It was good to set **paw** on Earth again!

BACK ON EARTH!

When the astromice returned to Earth, the world's journalists were waiting, eager to hear their stories and to see the FILMS and photographs of the most mouserific ADVENTURE of the century.

Before Greta Van Rodenten even removed her SPACE SUIT, she began making phone calls, trying to sell memories of her trip to the highest bidder.

"Did you get a picture of Professor Golden while he was vandalizing the **robots**?" everyone wanted to know.

But only **Newsmouse** and Focus had images of the great SCOOP, not Greta!

Newsmouse and Focus insisted that the biggest magazines and websites publish accounts written by the THEA SISTERS.

"These mouselets are absolutely brilliant journalists!" they assured their editors. "And it's all thanks to them that we have returned safe and sound—and that we have become friends again."

Napoleon Smith thanked the THEA SISTERS for all they had done. "Thank you for saving TITANIA! Ask me for anything you want and it's yours!"

"There is ONE thing," Nicky said with DETERMINATION. "You must promise to find a way to dispose of that SPACE JUNK! Some of that stuff was tossed out there by your robots."

"You're right!" Mr. Smith admitted regretfully. "That will be the first thing I do. I have experienced firsthand just how DANGEROUS that trash can be!"

The mouselets' return to MOUSEFORD ACADEMY was triumphant. All of WHALE ISLAND was decorated.

Midge Whale, the academy's cook, had baked an enormouse cake shaped like the moon with a chocolate space shuttle on top!

I was the first one to greet the mouselets.

"THEA!" they squealed as I threw my PAWS around them.

WELCOME
THEA SISTERS

"I am so proud of you!" I exclaimed. "You mouselets are truly lunar luminaries!"

"We can't wait to tell you about our trip!" Nicky cried.

"This time you've really **outdone** yourselves!" I told them. "You were **out of this world**!"

Want to read the next adventure of the Thea Sisters? I can't wait to tell you all about it!

THEA STILTON
BIG TROUBLE IN THE BIG APPLE

The Thea Sisters are off to New York City for another fabumouse adventure! Nicky has been training to run the Big Apple Marathon, and her friends are there to support her. While in the city, they visit Pamela's family and have a delicious dinner at the family's pizzeria. But someone has been threatening to burn the restaurant down, and Pam's family might have to close it for good to stay safe! Will the Thea Sisters catch this troublemaker before it's too late?

And don't miss any of my other fabumouse adventures!

THEA STILTON AND THE DRAGON'S CODE

THEA STILTON AND THE MOUNTAIN OF FIRE

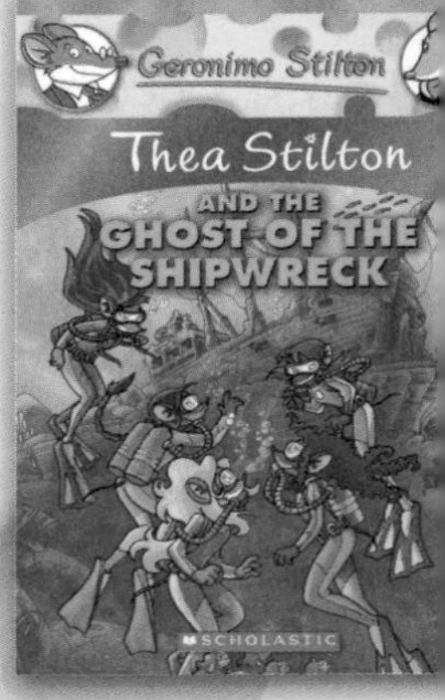

THEA STILTON AND THE GHOST O THE SHIPWRECK

THEA STILTON AND THE SECRET CITY

THEA STILTON AND THE MYSTERY IN PARIS

THEA STILTON AND THE CHERRY BLOSSOM ADVENTU

Want to read my next adventure?
I can't wait to tell you all about it!

THE HAUNTED CASTLE

I was just minding my business at home when I got a telephone call. It was my uncle Samuel S. Stingysnout, inviting the whole Stilton family to creepy, faraway Penny Pincher Castle for a big surprise. Moldy mozzarella! I'm not much of a traveling mouse, and I hate surprises. But Thea, Trap, and Benjamin were going, so I couldn't say no. I could tell this was going to be one super-spooky trip!

#1 LOST TREASURE OF THE EMERALD EYE

#2 THE CURSE OF THE CHEESE PYRAMID

#3 CAT AND MOUSE IN A HAUNTED HOUSE

#4 I'M TOO FO
OF MY FUR!

#5 FOUR MICE DEEP IN THE JUNGLE

#6 PAWS OFF, CHEDDARFACE!

#7 RED PIZZAS FOR A BLUE COUNT

#8 ATTACK O
THE BANDIT C

#9 A FABUMOUSE VACATION FOR GERONIMO

#10 ALL BECAUSE OF A CUP OF COFFEE

#11 IT'S HALLOWEEN, YOU 'FRAIDY MOUSE!

#12 MERRY CHRISTMAS, GERONIMO!

#13 THE PHANTOM OF THE SUBWAY

#14 THE TEMPLE OF THE RUBY OF FIRE

#15 THE MONA MOUSA CODE

#16 A CHEES
COLORED CAM

#17 WATCH
UR WHISKERS,
STILTON!

#18 SHIPWRECK ON
THE PIRATE ISLANDS

#19 MY NAME
IS STILTON,
GERONIMO STILTON

#20 SURF'S UP,
GERONIMO!

21 THE WILD,
WILD WEST

#22 THE SECRET
OF CACKLEFUR
CASTLE

A CHRISTMAS
TALE

#23 VALENTINE'S
DAY DISASTER

FIELD TRIP TO
AGARA FALLS

#25 THE SEARCH
FOR SUNKEN
TREASURE

#26 THE MUMMY
WITH NO NAME

#27 THE CHRISTMAS
TOY FACTORY

28 WEDDING
CRASHER

#29 DOWN AND OUT
DOWN UNDER

#30 THE MOUSE
ISLAND MARATHON

#31 THE MYSTERIOUS
CHEESE THIEF

CHRISTMAS CATASTROPHE

#32 VALLEY OF THE GIANT SKELETONS

#33 GERONIMO AND THE GOLD MEDAL MYSTERY

#34 GERONI STILTON, SEC AGENT

#35 A VERY MERRY CHRISTMAS

#36 GERONIMO'S VALENTINE

#37 THE RACE ACROSS AMERICA

#38 A FABUMO SCHOOL ADVENTURE

#39 SINGING SENSATION

#40 THE KARATE MOUSE

#41 MIGHTY MOUNT KILIMANJARO

#42 THE PECUL PUMPKIN THIE

#43 I'M NOT A SUPERMOUSE!

#44 THE GIANT DIAMOND ROBBERY

#45 SAVE THE WHITE WHALE!

Coming soon!

#46 THE HAUNTED CAS

Meet

CREEPELLA VON CACKLEFUR

I, *Geronimo Stilton*, have a lot of mouse friends, but none as **spooky** as my friend CREEPELLA VON CACKLEFUR! She is an enchanting and MYSTERIOUS mouse with a pet bat named **Bitewing**. YIKES! I'm a real 'fraidy mouse, but even I think CREEPELLA and her family are AWFULLY fascinating. I can't wait for you to read all about CREEPELLA in these fa-mouse-ly funny and **spectacularly spooky** tales!

#1 THE THIRTEEN GHOSTS

#2 MEET ME IN HORRORWOOD

THANKS FOR READING, AND GOOD-BYE UNTIL OUR NEXT ADVENTURE!

Thea Sisters